Oi Puppies!

Written by
Kes Gray

Illustrated by
Jim Field

h
Hodder
Children's
Books

"How many puppies?" frowned the frog.

"Quite a lot of puppies," gulped the dog.

"Why won't they **SIT?**" asked the cat.

"Because they're puppies," said the dog.
"Puppies are far too busy being puppies to sit."

"There's a puppy hanging from my whiskers,"
frowned the cat.

"He's called
Spot,"
said the dog.

"There's a puppy chewing my swimming trunks,"
said the frog.

"She's called **Lollie,**"
said the dog.

"What are *these* puppies called?"
asked the frog.

"**Tickle, Blue, Scamp, Rebel, Smudge**
and **Shep**," said the dog.

"And what are *these* puppies called?" frowned the cat.

"**Winnie, Cheeky, Spike, Flash, Trubble,** and **Trixie,**" said the dog.

"WELL, DO SOMETHING ABOUT THEM!"

yelled the cat.

"Let me make a phone call," said the frog.

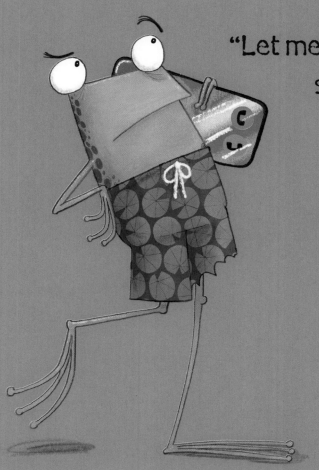

"Where do you want everything?"
said the delivery duck.

"On the next page,
please," said the frog.

"I wonder what **Spot** is sitting on?" said the dog.

Scamp's
on a
lamp,

Cheeky is on some
tzatziki,

and
Blue's
on a
shoe."

"I wonder what **Lollie** is sitting on?" said the cat.

"**Lollie's** on a **trolley**," said the frog.

"**Lollie's** on a **trolley**,

Trixie's on a **pixie**,

Flash
is on a
splash,

Spike's
on a
trike,

Winnie's
on a
pinny,

and

Trubble
is
on
a
bubble."

"I've never seen so many puppies
SO well behaved."

"Hold on, what do **tadpoles** sit on?" said the dog.

"And **kittens** that are **allergic** to **mittens?**" said the cat.

"WHY DO YOU ASK?"

frowned the frog.

"OI TAXI!"
yelled the frog.
"MY NAME IS ORANGE!"
"MY NAME IS LEMON!"
'M MIFFYMOPS!"
"I'M CUTEYKINS!"
"MY NAME IS DIDDLY!"
"MY NAME IS SQUIGGLY!"

To Dexter, Amanda and Lottie K.G.
For the libraries and the librarians. Thank you! J.F.

HODDER CHILDREN'S BOOKS
First published in Great Britain in 2019 by Hodder and Stoughton

A CIP catalogue record for this book is available from the British Library.

ISBN: 978 1 444 93735 0

3 5 7 9 10 8 6 4 2

Printed and bound in China

Hodder Children's Books
An imprint of Hachette Children's Group
Part of Hodder and Stoughton
Carmelite House, 50 Victoria Embankment
London, EC4Y 0DZ

An Hachette UK Company
www.hachette.co.uk
www.hachettechildrens.co.uk

www.kesgray.com
www.jimfield.co.uk